MARK TATULLI

THEY CAME

ROARING BROOK PRESS
NEW YORK

They.

They came.

Across the far reaches of inky space, past the glow of planets and sparkly stars.

The giant machine roared and hissed.

It tweeted and creaked.

It made all manner of mysterious sounds as it rolled into position for landing.

The heavy metal feet hit the ground, shaking bicycle frames and spilling cups of juice.

He ordered his officers to surround the great spacecraft with yards and yards of STAND-BACK-AND-DO-NOT-TOUCH tape.

She directed that bright lights be plugged in and cameras be focused on the huge, motionless machine.

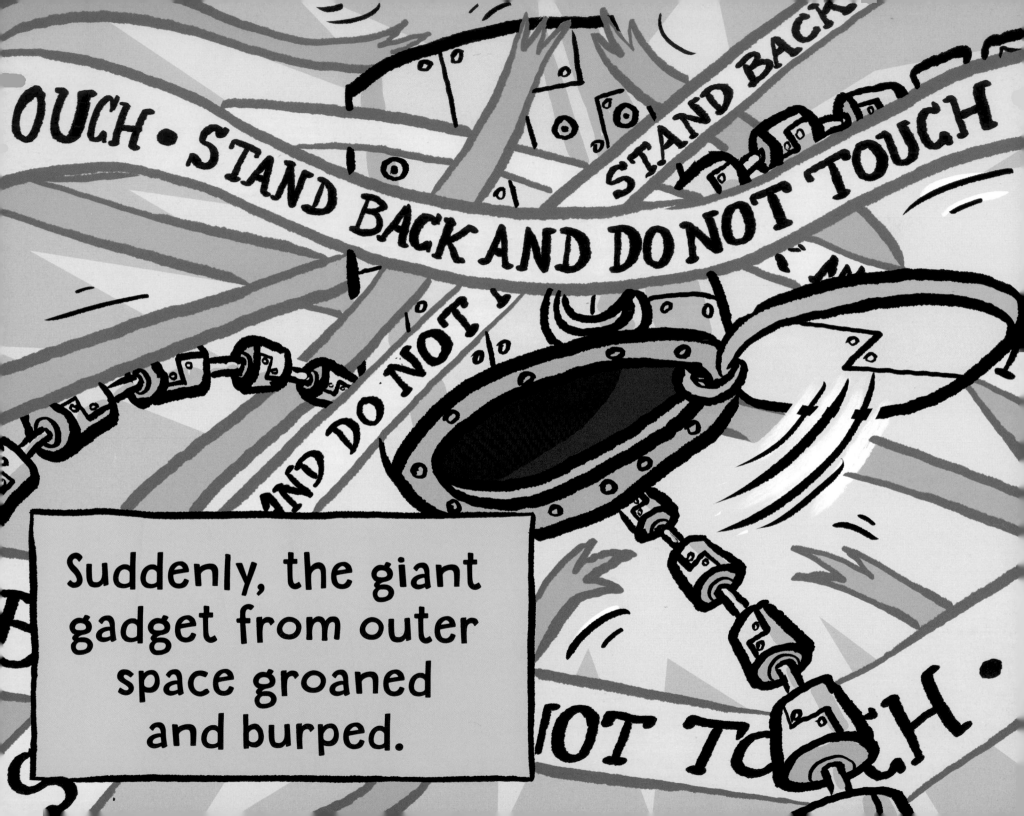

Suddenly, the giant gadget from outer space groaned and burped.

Then something like a door popped open.

It was Stephen Sprout, the smallish kid
from Garnet Lane—

—who wasn't big enough for a two-wheeler and was rumored to sleep with a night-light.

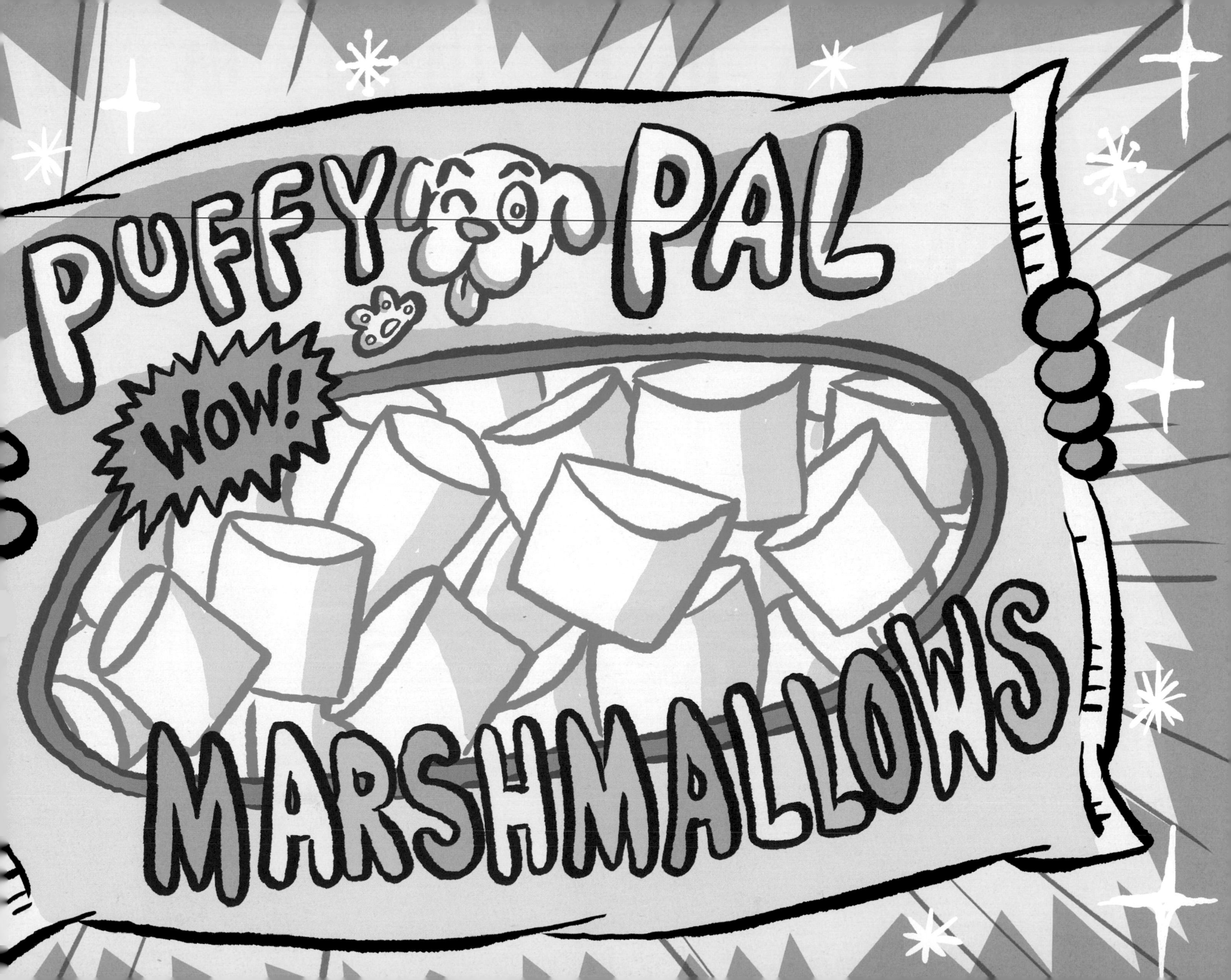
PUFFY PAL
WOW!
MARSHMALLOWS

Just then a great rubber tube sprang from the spaceship's open door...

and stopped right where Stephen stood.

At the end of the tube was a metal box—

—and on the metal box, a small door.

And Stephen knew just what it was missing.

The Great Marshmallow and Hot Chocolate Picnic

To Dan, Connie, and Andrew—without whom this book might have bounced around in my head forever. My many thanks.

Copyright © 2018 by Mark Tatulli
Published by Roaring Brook Press
Roaring Brook Press is a division of Holtzbrinck Publishing Holdings Limited Partnership
175 Fifth Avenue, New York, NY 10010
mackids.com

Library of Congress Control Number: 2017957303
ISBN: 978-1-62672-355-9

Our books may be purchased in bulk for promotional, educational, or business use. Please contact your local bookseller or the Macmillan Corporate and Premium Sales Department at (800) 221-7945 ext. 5442 or by e-mail at MacmillanSpecialMarkets@macmillan.com.

First edition, 2018
Book design by Andrew Arnold
Color separations by Embassy Graphics
Printed in China by RR Donnelley Asia Printing Solutions, Ltd., Dongguan City, Guangdong Province

10 9 8 7 6 5 4 3 2 1